Poems of Optimism

Ella Wheeler Wilcox

Poems of Optimism

War

Greater Britain
Belgium
Knitting
Mobilisation
Neutral
A book for the King
The men-made gods
The Ghosts
The poet's theme
Europe
After
The Peace Angel
Peace should not come

Miscellaneous

The Winds of Fate
Beauty
The invisible helpers
To the women of Australia
Replies
Earth bound
A Successful Man
Unsatisfied
Separation
To the teachers of the young
Beauty making
On Avon's breast I saw a stately swan
The little go-cart
I am running forth to meet you

The second coming

Our hearts were not set on fighting,
  We did not pant for the fray,
And whatever wrongs need righting,
  We would not have met that way.
But the way that has opened before us
  Leads on thro' a blood-red field;
And we swear by the great God o'er us,
  We will die, but we will not yield.

The battle is not of our making,
  And war was never our plan;
Yet, all that is sweet forsaking,
  We march to it, man by man.
It is either to smite, or be smitten,
  There's no other choice to-day;
And we live, as befits the Briton,
  Or we die, as the Briton may.

We were not fashioned for cages,
  Or to feed from a keeper's hand;
Our strength which has grown thro' ages
  Is the strength of a slave-free land.
We cannot kneel down to a master,
  To our God alone can we pray;
And we stand in this world disaster,
  To fight, like a lion at bay.

For works with similar titles, see Belgium.

     Ruined? destroyed? Ah, no; though blood in rivers ran
Down all her ancient streets; though treasures manifold
Love-wrought, Time-mellowed, and beyond the price of gold
Are lost, yet Belgium's star shines still in God's vast plan.

Rarely have Kings been great, since kingdoms first began;
Rarely have great kings been great men, when all was told.
But, by the lighted torch in mailèd hands, behold,
Immortal Belgium's immortal king, and Man.

At the concert and the play
Everywhere you see them sitting,
Knitting, knitting.
Women who the other day
Thought of nothing but their frocks
Or their jewels or their locks,
Women who have lived for pleasure,
Who have known no work but leisure,
Now are knitting, knitting, knitting
For the soldiers over there.

On the trains and on the ships
With a diligence befitting,
They are knitting.
Some with smiles upon their lips,
Some with manners debonair,
Some with earnest look and air.
But each heart in its own fashion,
Weaves in pity and compassion
In their knitting, knitting, knitting
For the soldiers over there.

Hurried women to and fro
From their homes to labour flitting,
Knitting, knitting,
Busy handed come and go.
Broken bits of time they spare,
Just to feel they do their share,
Just to keep life's sense of beauty
In the doing of a duty,
They are knitting, knitting, knitting
For the soldiers over there.

Oh the Kings of earth have mobilised their men.
See them moving, valour proving,
To the fields of glory going,
Banners flowing, bugles blowing,
Every one a mother's son,
Brave with uniform and gun,
Keeping step with easy swing,
Yes, with easy step and light marching onward to the fight,
Just to please the warlike fancy of a King;
Who has mobilised his army for the strife.

Oh the King of Death has mobilised his men.
See the hearses huge and black
How they rumble down the track;
With their coffins filled with dead,
Filled with men who fought and bled;
Now from fields of glory coming
To the sound of muffled drumming
They are lying still and white,
But the Kings have had their fight;
Death has mobilised his army for the grave.

That pale word 'Neutral' sits becomingly
On lips of weaklings. But the men whose brains
Find fuel in their blood, the men whose minds
Hold sympathetic converse with their hearts,
Such men are never neutral. That word stands
Unsexed and impotent in Realms of Speech.
When mighty problems face a startled world
No virile man is neutral. Right or wrong
His thoughts go forth, assertive, unafraid
To stand by his convictions, and to do
Their part in shaping issues to an end.
Silence may guard the door of useless words,
At dictate of Discretion; but to stand
Without opinions in a world which needs
Constructive thinking, is a coward's part.

A book has been made for the King,
A book of beauty and art;
To the good king's eyes
A smile shall rise
Hiding the ache in his heart -
Hiding the hurt and the grief
As he turns it, leaf by leaf.

A book has been made for the King,
A book of blood and of blight;
To the Great King's eyes
A look shall rise
That will blast and wither and smite -
Yes, smite with a just God's rage,
As He turns it, page by page.

Said the Kaiser's god to the god of the Czar:
  'Hark, hark, how my people pray.
Their faith, methinks, is greater by far
Than all the faiths of the others are;
  They know I will help them slay.'

Said the god of the Czar: 'My people call
  In a medley of tongues; they know
I will lend my strength to them one and all.
Wherever they fight their foes shall fall
  Like grass where the mowers go.'

Then the god of the Gauls spoke out of a cloud
  To the god of the King nearby:
'Our people pray, tho' they pray not loud;
They ask for courage to slaughter a crowd,
  And to laugh, tho' themselves may die.'

And far out into the heart of Space
  Where a lonely pathway crept,
Up over the stars, to a secret place,
Where no light shone but the light of His face,
  Christ covered His eyes and wept.

For works with similar titles, see The Ghosts.

There was no wind, and yet the air
  Seemed suddenly astir;
There were no forms, and yet all space
  Seemed thronged with growing hosts.
They came from Where, and from Nowhere,
  Like phantoms as they were;
They came from many a land and place -
  The ghosts, the ghosts, the ghosts.

And some were white, and some were grey,
  And some were red as blood -
Those ghosts of men who met their death
  Upon the field of war.
Against the skies of fading day,
  Like banks of cloud they stood;
And each wraith asked another wraith,
  'What were we fighting for?'

One said, 'I was my mother's all;
  And she was old and blind.'
Another, 'Back on earth, my wife
  And week-old baby lie.'
Another, 'At the bugle's call,
  I left my bride behind;
Love made so beautiful my life
  I could not bear to die.'

In voices like the winds that moan
  Among pine trees at night,
They whispered long, the newly dead,
  While listening stars came out.
'We wonder if the cause is known,
  And if the war was right,
That killed us in our prime,' they said,
  'And what it was about.'

They came in throngs that filled all space -
  Those whispering phantom hosts;
They came from many a land and place,
  The ghosts, the ghosts, the ghosts.

Why should the poet of these pregnant times
Be asked to sing of war's unholy crimes?

To laud and eulogise the trade which thrives
On horrid holocausts of human lives?

Man was a fighting beast when earth was young,
And war the only theme when Homer sung.

'Twixt might and might the equal contest lay:
Not so the battles of our modern day.

Too often now the conquering hero struts,
A Gulliver among the Lilliputs.

Success no longer rests on skill or fate,
But on the movements of a syndicate.

Of old, men fought and deemed it right and just,
To-day the warrior fights because he must;

And in his secret soul feels shame because
He desecrates the higher manhood's laws.

Oh, there are worthier themes for poet's pen
In this great hour than bloody deeds of men:

The rights of many - not the worth of one -
The coming issues, not the battle done;

The awful opulence and awful need -
The rise of brotherhood - the fall of greed;

The soul of man replete with God's own force,
The call 'to heights,' and not the cry 'to horse.'

Are there not better themes in this great age
For pen of poet, or for voice of sage,

Than those old tales of killing? Song is dumb
Only that greater song in time may come.

When comes the bard, he whom the world waits for,
He will not sing of War.

For works with similar titles, see Europe.
> Little lads and grandsires,
Women old with care;
But all the men are dying men
Or dead men over there.

No one stops to dig graves;
Who has time to spare?
The dead men, the dead men
How the dead men stare.

Kings are out a-hunting -
Oh, the sport is rare;
With dying men and dead men
Falling everywhere.

Life for lads and grandsires;
Spoils for kings to share;
And dead men, dead men,
Dead men everywhere.

For works with similar titles, see After.

     Over the din of battle,
Over the cannons' rattle,
Over the strident voices of men and their dying groans,
I hear the falling of thrones.

Out of the wild disorder
That spreads from border to border,
I see a new world rising from ashes of ancient towns;
And the Rulers wear no crowns.

Over the blood-charged water,
Over the fields of slaughter,
Down to the hidden vaults of Time, where lie the worn-out things
I see the passing of Kings.

Angel of Peace, the hounds of war,
Unleashed, are all abroad,
And war's foul trade again is made
    Man's leading aim in life.
Blood dyes the billow and the sod;
    The very winds are rife
With tales of slaughter. Angel, pray,
What can we do or think or say
In times like these?
    'Child, think of God!'

'Before this little speck in space
Called Earth with light was shod,
Great chains and tiers of splendid spheres
    Were fashioned by His hand.
Be thine the part to love and laud,
    Nor seek to understand.
Go lift thine eyes from death-charged guns
To one who made a billion suns;
And trust and wait.
    Child, dwell on God!'

Peace should not come along this foul, earth way.
Peace should not come, until we cleanse the path.
God waited for us; now in awful wrath
He pours the blood of men out day by day
To purify the highroad for her feet.
Why, what would Peace do, in a world where hearts
Are filled with thoughts like poison-pointed darts?
It were not meet, surely it were not meet
For Peace to come, and with her white robes hide
These industries of death - these guns and swords, -
These uniformed, hate-filled, destructive hordes, -
These hideous things, that are each nation's pride.
So long as men believe in armèd might
Let arms be brandished. Let not Peace be sought
Until the race-heart empties out all thought
Of blows and blood, as arguments for Right.
The world has never had enough of war,
Else war were not. Now let the monster stand,
Until he slays himself with his own hand;
Though no man knows what he is fighting for.
Then in the place where wicked cannons stood
Let Peace erect her shrine of Brotherhood.

One ship drives east and another drives west,
With the self-same winds that blow,
  'Tis the set of the sails
  And not the gales
That tell them the way to go.
Like the winds of the sea are the winds of fate,
As we voyage along through life,
  'Tis the set of the soul
  That decides its goal
And not the calm or the strife.

For works with similar titles, see Beauty.

The search for beauty is the search for God
Who is All Beauty. He who seeks shall find.
And all along the paths my feet have trod,
I have sought hungrily with heart and mind,
    And open eyes for beauty, everywhere.
    Lo! I have found the world is very fair.
The search for beauty is the search for God.

Beauty was first revealed to me by stars,
    Before I saw it in my mother's eyes,
Or, seeing, sensed it beauty, I was stirred
To awe and wonder by those orbs of light
    All palpitant against empurpled skies.
They spoke a language to my childish heart
Of mystery and splendour, and of space,
Friendly with gracious, unseen presences.
Beauty was first revealed to me by stars.

Sunsets enlarged the meaning of the word.
    There was a window looking to the west;
Beyond it, wide Wisconsin fields of grain,
And then a hill, whereon white flocks of clouds
    Would gather in the afternoon to rest.
And when the sun went down behind that hill
What scenes of glory spread before my sight;
What beauty - beauty, absolute, supreme!
Sunsets enlarged the meaning of that word.

Clover in blossom, red and honey-sweet,
    In summer billowed like a crimson sea
Across the meadow lands. One day, I stood
Breast-high amidst its waves, and heard the hum
    Of myriad bees, that had gone mad like me
With fragrance and with beauty. Over us,
A loving sun smiled from a cloudless sky,
While a bold breeze kissed lightly as it passed,

Clover in blossom, red and honey-sweet.

Autumn spoke loudly of the beautiful.
  And in the gallery of Nature hung
Colossal pictures hard against the sky,
Set forests gorgeous with a hundred hues;
  And with each morning, some new wonder flung
Before the startled world; some daring shade,
Some strange, new scheme of colour and of form.
Autumn spoke loudly of the beautiful.

Winter, though rude, is delicate in art -
  More delicate than Summer or than fall
(Even as rugged man is more refined
In vital things than woman). Winter's touch
  On Nature seemed most beautiful of all -
That evanescent beauty of the frost
On window panes; of clean, fresh, fallen snow;
Of white, white sunlight on the ice-draped trees.
Winter, though rude, is delicate in art.

Morning! The word itself is beautiful,
  And the young hours have many gifts to give
That feed the soul with beauty. He who keeps
His days for labour and his nights for sleep
  Wakes conscious of the joy it is to live,
And brings from that mysterious Land of Dreams
A sense of beauty that illumines earth.
Morning! The word itself is beautiful.

The search for beauty is the search for God.

There are, there are
Invisible Great Helpers of the race.
Across unatlased continents of space,
From star to star.
   In answer to some soul's imperious need,
   They speed, they speed.

When the earth-loving young are forced to stand
Upon the border of the Unknown Land,
They come, they come - those angels who have trod
The altitudes of God,
And to the trembling heart
Their strength impart.
   Have you not seen the delicate young maid,
Filled with the joy of life in her fair dawn,
   Look in the face of death, all unafraid,
And smilingly pass on?

This is not human strength; not even faith
   Has such large confidence in such an hour.
   It is a power
Supplied by beings who have conquered death.
   Floating from sphere to sphere
   They hover near
The souls that need the courage they can give.

This is no vision of a dreamer's mind.
Though we are blind
They live, they live,
Filling all space -
Invisible Great Helpers of the race.

A toast to the splendid daughters
Of the New World over the waters,
  A world that is great as new;
Daughters of brave old races,
Daughters of heights and spaces,
Broad seas and broad earth places -
  Hail to your land and you!

The sun and the winds have fed you;
The width of your world has led you
  Out into the larger view;
Strong with a strength that is tender,
Bright with a primal splendour,
Homage and praise we render -
  Hail to your land and you!

Sisters and daughters and mothers,
Standing abreast with your brothers,
  Working for things that are true;
Thinking and doing and daring,
Giving, receiving, and sharing,
Earning the crowns you are wearing -
  Hail to your land and you!

You have lived long and learned the secret of life, O
Seer!
Tell me what are the best three things to seek -
The best three things for a man to seek on earth?

The best three things for a man to seek, O Son! are these:
Reverence for that great Source from whence he came;
Work for the world wherein he finds himself;
And knowledge of the Realm toward which he goes.

What are the best three things to love on earth, O Seer!
What are the best three things for a man to love?

The best three things for a man to love, O Son! are these:
Labour which keeps his forces all in action;
A home wherein no evil thing may enter;
And a loving woman with God in her heart.

What are the three great sins to shun, O Seer! -
What are the three great sins for a man to shun?

The three great sins for a man to shun, O Son! are these:
A thought which soils the heart from whence it goes;
An action that can harm a living thing;
And undeveloped energies of mind.

What are the worst three things to fear, O Seer! -
What are the worst three things for a man to fear?

The worst three things for man to fear, O Son! are these:
Doubt and suspicion in a young child's eyes;
Accusing shame upon a woman's face;
And in himself no consciousness of God.

New paradise, and groom and bride;
The world was all their own;
Her heart swelled full of love and pride;
Yet were they quite alone?
'Now how is it, oh how is it, and why is it' (in fear
All silent to herself she spake) 'that something strange seems
here?'

Along the garden paths they walked -
The moon was at its height -
And lover-wise they strolled and talked,
But something was not right.
And 'Who is that, now who is that, oh who is that,' quoth she,
(All silent in her heart she spake) 'that seems to follow me?'

He drew her closer to his side;
She felt his lingering kiss;
And yet a shadow seemed to glide
Between her heart and his.
And 'What is that, now what is that, oh what is that,' she said,
(All silent to herself she spake) 'that minds me of the dead?'

They wandered back by beds of bloom;
They climbed a winding stair;
They crossed the threshold of their room,
But something waited there.
'Now who is this, and what is this, and where is this,' she
cried,
(All silent was the cry she made) 'that comes to haunt and
hide?'

Wide-eyed she lay, the while he slept;
She could not name her fear.
But something from her bedside crept
Just as the dawn drew near,
(She did not know, she could not know - how could she

know? - who came
 To haunt the home of one whose hand had dug her grave of
shame).

There was a man who killed a loving maid
In some mad mood of passion; and he paid
The price, upon a scaffold. Now his name
Stands only as a synonym for shame.
There was another man, who took to wife
A loving woman. She was full of life,
Of hope, and aspirations; and her pride
Clothed her like some rich mantle.

First, the wide
Glad stream of life that through her veins had sway
He dammed by rocks, cast in it, day by day.
Her flag of hope, flung gaily to the world,
He placed half mast, and then hauled down, and furled.
The aspirations, breathing in each word,
By subtle ridicule, were made absurd:

The delicate fine mantle of her pride,
With rude unfeeling hands, was wrenched aside:
And by mean avarice, or vulgar show,
Her quivering woman's heart was made to know
That she was but a chattel, bought to fill
Whatever niche might please the buyer's will.

So she was murdered, while the slow years went.
And her assassin, honoured, opulent,
Lived with no punishment, or social ban!
'A good provider, a successful man.'

The bird flies home to its young;
The flower folds its leaves about an opening bud;
And in my neighbour's house there is the cry of a child.
I close my window that I need not hear.

She is mine, and she is very beautiful:
And in her heart there is no evil thought.
There is even love in her heart -
Love of life, love of joy, love of this fair world,
And love of me (or love of my love for her);
Yet she will never consent to bear me a child.
And when I speak of it she weeps,
Always she weeps, saying:
'Do I not bring joy enough into your life?
Are you not satisfied with me and my love,
As I am satisfied with you?
Never would I urge you to some great peril
To please my whim; yet ever so you urge me,
Urge me to risk my happiness - yea, life itself -
So lightly do you hold me.' And then she weeps,
Always she weeps, until I kiss away her tears
And soothe her with sweet lies, saying I am content.
Then she goes singing through the house like some bright
bird
Preening her wings, making herself all beautiful,
Perching upon my knee, and pecking at my lips
With little kisses. So again love's ship
Goes sailing forth upon a portless sea,
From nowhere unto nowhere; and it takes
Or brings no cargoes to enrich the world.

The years
Are passing by us. We will yet be old
Who now are young. And all the man in me
Cries for the reproduction of myself
Through her I love. Why, love and youth like ours

Could populate with gods and goddesses
This great, green earth, and give the race new types
Were it made fruitful! Often I can see,
As in a vision, desolate old age
And loneliness descending on us two,
And nowhere in the world, nowhere beyond the earth,
Fruit of my loins and of her womb to feed
Our hungry hearts. To me it seems
More sorrowful than sitting by small graves
And wetting sad-eyed pansies with our tears.

The bird flies home to its young;
The flower folds its leaves about an opening bud;
And in my neighbour's house there is the cry of a child.
I close my window that I need not hear.

One decade and a half since first we came
With hearts aflame
Into Love's Paradise, as man and mate;
And now we separate.
Soon, all too soon,
Waned the white splendour of our honeymoon.
  We saw it fading; but we did not know
   How bleak the path would be when once its glow
Was wholly gone.
And yet we two were forced to follow on -
  Leagues, leagues apart while ever side by side.
    Darker and darker grew the loveless weather,
Darker the way,
Until we could not stay
   Longer together.
  Now that all anger from our hearts has died,
And love has flown far from its ruined nest,
To find sweet shelter in another breast,
  Let us talk calmly of our past mistakes,
   And of our faults; if only for the sakes
Of those with whom our futures will be cast.
  You shall speak first.

SHE

A woman would speak last -
  Tell me my first grave error as a wife.

HE

  Inertia. My young veins were rife
With manhood's ardent blood; and love was fire
Within me. But you met my strong desire
  With lips like frozen rose leaves - chaste, so chaste

That all your splendid beauty seemed but waste
Of love's materials. Then of that beauty
   Which had so pleased my sight
You seemed to take no care; you felt no duty
   To keep yourself an object of delight
   For lover's-eyes; and appetite
And indolence soon wrought
Their devastating changes. You were not
   The woman I had sworn to love and cherish.
If love is starved, what can love do but perish?
Now will you speak of my first fatal sin
   And all that followed, even as I have done?

SHE

I must begin
   With the young quarter of our honeymoon.
  You are but one
   Of countless men who take the priceless boon
Of woman's love and kill it at the start,
   Not wantonly but blindly. Woman's passion
Is such a subtle thing - woof of her heart,
Web of her spirit; and the body's part
  Is to play ever but the lesser rôle
  To her white soul.
   Seized in brute fashion,
It fades like down on wings of butterflies;
Then dies.
  So my love died.
  Next, on base Mammon's cross you nailed my pride,
  Making me ask for what was mine by right:
  Until, in my own sight,
  I seemed a helpless slave
  To whom the master gave
A grudging dole. Oh, yes, at times gifts showered
Upon your chattel; but I was not dowered

By generous love. Hate never framed a curse
Or placed a cruel ban
That so crushed woman, as the law of man
    That makes her pensioner upon his purse.
That necessary stuff called gold is such
A cold, rude thing it needs the nicest touch
    Of thought and speech when it approaches love,
    Or it will prove the certain death thereof.

HE

Your words cut deep; 'tis time we separate.

SHE

Well, each goes wiser to a newer mate.

How large thy task, O teacher of the young,
To take the ravelled threads by parents flung
With careless hands, and through consummate care
To weave a fabric, fine and firm and fair.
God's uncompleted work is thine to do -
Be brave and true!

Methinks there is no greater work in life
Than making beauty. Can the mind conceive
One little corner in celestial realms
Unbeautiful, or dull or commonplace?
Or picture ugly angels, illy clad?
Beauty and splendour, opulence and joy,
Are attributes of God and His domain,
And so are worth and virtue. But why preach
Of virtue only to the sons of men,
Ignoring beauty, till they think it sin?
Why, if each dweller on this little globe
Could know the sacred meaning of that word
And understand its deep significance,
Men's thoughts would form in beauty, till their dreams
Of heaven would find expression in their lives,
However humble; they themselves would grow
Godlike, befitting such a fair estate.
Let us be done with what is only good,
Demanding here and now the beautiful;
Lest, with the mind and eye on earth untrained,
We shall be ill at ease when heaven is gained.

One day when England's June was at its best,
I saw a stately and imperious swan
Floating on Avon's fair untroubled breast.
Sudden, it seemed as if all strife had gone
Out of the world; all discord, all unrest.

The sorrows and the sinnings of the race
Faded away like nightmares in the dawn.
All heaven was one blue background for the grace
Of Avon's beautiful, slow-moving swan;
And earth held nothing mean or commonplace.

Life seemed no longer to be hurrying on
With unbecoming haste; but softly trod,
As one who reads in emerald leaf, or lawn,
Or crimson rose a message straight from God.
.....
On Avon's breast I saw a stately swan.

It was long, long ago that a soul like a flower
Unfolded, and blossomed, and passed in an hour.
It was long, long ago; and the memory seems
Like the pleasures and sorrows that come in our dreams.

The kind years have crowned me with many a joy
Since the going away of my wee little boy;
Each one as it passed me has stooped with a kiss,
And left some delight - knowing one thing I miss.

But when in the park or the street, all elate
A baby I see in his carriage of state,
As proud as a king, in his little go-cart -
I feel all the mother-love stir in my heart!

And I seem to be back in that long-vanished May;
And the baby, who came but to hurry away
In the little white hearse, is not dead, but alive,
And out in his little go-cart for a drive.

I whisper a prayer as he rides down the street,
And my thoughts follow after him, tender and sweet;
For I know, by a law that is vast and divine,
(Though I know not his name) that the baby is mine!

I am running forth to meet you, O my Master,
For they tell me you are surely on the way;
Yes, they tell me you are coming back again
(While I run, while I run).
And I wish my feet were winged to speed on faster,
And I wish I might behold you here to-day,
Lord of men.

I am running, yet I walk beside my neighbour,
And I take the duties given me to do;
Yes, I take the daily duties as they fall
(While I run, while I run),
And my heart runs to my hand and helps the labour,
For I think this is the way that leads to you,
Lord of all.

I am running, yet I turn from toil and duty,
Oftentimes to just the art of being glad;
Yes, to just the joys that make the earth-world bright
(While I run, while I run).
For the soul that worships God must worship beauty,
And the heart that thinks of You can not be sad,
Lord of light.

I am running, yet I pause to greet my brother,
And I lean to rid my garden of its weed;
Yes, I lean, although I lift my thoughts above
(While I run, while I run).
And I think of that command, 'Love one another,'
As I hear discordant sounds of creed with creed,
Lord of Love.

I am running, and the road is lit with splendour,
And it brightens and shines fairer with each span;
Yes, it brightens like the highway in a dream
(While I run, while I run).

And my heart to all the world grows very tender,
For I seem to see the Christ in every man,
Lord supreme.

Fame writes ever its song and story,
For heroes of war, in letters of glory.

But where is the story and where is the song
For the heroes of peace and the martyrs of wrong?

They fight their battles in shop and mine;
They die at their posts and make no sign.

They herd like beasts in a slaughter pen;
They live like cattle and suffer like men.

Why, set by the horrors of such a life,
Like a merry-go-round seems the battle's strife,

And the open sea, and the open boat,
And the deadly cannon with bellowing throat.

Oh, what are they all, with death thrown in,
To the life that has nothing to lose or win -

The life that has nothing to hope or gain
But ill-paid labour and beds of pain?

Fame, where is your story and where is your song
For the martyrs of peace and the victims of wrong?

For works with similar titles, see Home.   The greatest words
are always solitaires,
    Set singly in one syllable; like birth,
    Life, love, hope, peace. I sing the worth
Of that dear word toward which the whole world fares -
    I sing of home.

To make a home, we should take all of love
    And much of labour, patience, and keen joy;
    Then mix the elements of earth's alloy
With finer things drawn from the realms above,
    The spirit home.

There should be music, melody and song;
    Beauty in every spot; an open door
    And generous sharing of the pleasure store
With fellow-pilgrims as they pass along,
    Seeking for home.

Make ample room for silent friends - the books,
    That give so much and only ask for space.
    Nor let Utility crowd out the vase
Which has no use save gracing by its looks
    The precious home.

To narrow bounds let mirrors lend their aid
    And multiply each gracious touch of art;
    And let the casual stranger feel the part -
The great creative part - that love has played
    Within the home.

Here bring your best in thought and word and deed,
    Your sweetest acts, your highest self-control;
    Nor save them for some later hour and goal.
Here is the place, and now the time of need,
    Here in your home.

Time with his back against the mighty wall,
   Which hides from view all future joy and sorrow,
Hears, without answer, the impatient call
   Of puny man, to tell him of to-morrow.

Moral, be wise, and to the silence bow,
   These useless and unquiet ways forsaking;
Concern thyself with the Eternal Now -
   To-day hold all things, ready for thy taking.

If I were a man, a young man, and knew what I know
to-day,
  I would look in the eyes of Life undaunted
    By any Fate that might threaten me.
  I would give to the world what the world most wanted -
    Manhood that knows it can do and be;
    Courage that dares, and faith that can see
    Clear into the depths of the human soul,
    And find God there, and the ultimate goal,
If I were a man, a young man, and knew what I know to-day.

If I were a man, a young man, and knew what I know to-day,
  I would think of myself as the masterful creature
    Of all the Masterful plan;
  The Formless Cause, with form and feature;
    The Power that heeds not limit or ban;
    Man, wonderful man.
I would do good deeds, and forget them straightway;
  I would weave my woes into ropes and climb
Up to the heights of the helper's gateway;
    And Life should serve me, and Time,
    And I would sail out, and out, and find
    The treasures that lie in the deep sea, Mind.
  I would dream, and think, and act;
I would work, and love, and pray,
  Till each dream and vision grew into a fact,
If I were a man, a young man, and knew what I know to-day.

If I were a man, a young man, and knew what I know to-day,
  I would guard my passions as Kings guard treasures,
    And keep them high and clean.
  (For the will of a man, with his passions, measures;
    It is strong as they are keen.)
  I would think of each woman as some one's mother;
  I would think of each man as my own blood brother,
And speed him along on his way.

And the glory of life in this wonderful hour
Should fill me and thrill me with Conscious power,
If I were a man, a young man, and knew what I know to-day.

Now much there is need of doing must not be done in haste;
But slowly and with patience, as a jungle is changed to a town.
But listen, my brothers, listen; it is not always so:
When a murderer's hand is lifted to kill, there is no time to waste;
And the way to change his purpose is first to knock him down
And teach him the law of kindness after you give him the blow.

The acorn you plant in the morning will not give shade at noon;
And the thornless cactus must be bred by year on year of toil.
But listen, my brothers, listen; it is not ever the way,
For the roots of the poison ivy plant you cannot pull too soon;
If you would better your garden and make the most of your soil,
Hurry and dig up the evil things and cast them out to-day.

The ancient sin of the nations no law can ever efface;
We must wait for the mothers of men to grow, and give clean souls to their sons.
But listen, my brothers, listen - when a child cries out in pain,
We must rise from the banquet board and go, though the host is saying grace;
We must rise and find the Herod of Greed, who is killing our little ones,
Nor ever go back to the banquet until the monster is slain.

The strong man waits for justice, with lifted soul and eyes,
As a sturdy oak will face the storm, and does not break or bow.

But listen, my brothers, listen; the child is a child for a day;
If a merciless foot treads down each shoot, how can the forest
rise?

We are robbing the race when we rob a child; we must
rescue the children NOW;

We must rescue the little slaves of Greed and send them
out to play.

For works with similar titles, see Protest.   To sit in silence when
we should protest
Makes cowards out of men. The human race
Has climbed on protest. Had no voice been raised
Against injustice, ignorance and lust
The Inquisition yet would serve the law
And guillotines decide our least disputes.
The few who dare must speak and speak again
To right the wrongs of many. Speech, thank God,
No vested power in this great day and land
Can gag or throttle; Press and voice may cry
Loud disapproval of existing ills,
May criticise oppression and condemn
The lawlessness of wealth-protecting laws
That let the children and child-bearers toil
To purchase ease for idle millionaires,
Therefore do I protest against the boast
Of independence in this mighty land.
Call no chain strong which holds one rusted link,
Call no land free that holds one fettered slave
Until the manacled, slim wrists of babes
Are loosed to toss in childish sport and glee,
Until the Mother bears no burden save
The precious one beneath her heart; until
God's soil is rescued from the clutch of greed
And given back to labour, let no man
Call this the Land of Freedom.

Fate used me meanly; but I looked at her and laughed,
That none might know how bitter was the cup I quaffed.
Along came Joy, and paused beside me where I sat,
Saying, 'I came to see what you were laughing at.'

When the whole world resounds with rude alarms
Of warring arms,
When God's good earth, from border unto border
Shows man's disorder,
Let me not waste my dower of mortal might
In grieving over wrongs I cannot right.
This is my task: amid discordant strife
To keep a clean sweet centre in my life;
And though the human orchestra may be
Playing all out of key -
To tune my soul to symphonies above,
And sound the note of love.
This is my task.

When by the minds of men most beauteous Faith
Seems doomed to death,
And to her place is hoisted, by soul treason,
The dullard Reason,
Let me not hurry forth with flag unfurled
To proselyte an unbelieving world.
This is my task: in depths of unstarred night
Or in diverting and distracting light
To keep (in crowds, or in my room alone)
Faith on her lofty throne;
And whatsoever happen or befall,
To see God's hand in all.
This is my task.

When, in church pews, men worship God in words,
But meet their kind with swords,
When Fair Religion, stripped of holy passion,
Walks masked as Fashion,
Let me not wax indignant at the sight;
Or waste my strength bewailing her sad plight.
This is my task: to search in my own mind
Until the qualities of God I find;

To seek them in the hearts of friend and foe -
Or high or low;
And in my hours of toil, or prayer, or play,
To live my creed each day.
This is my task.

A granite rock in the mountain side
Gazed on the world and was satisfied.
It watched the centuries come and go,
It welcomed the sunlight yet loved the snow,
It grieved when the forest was forced to fall,
Yet joyed when steeples rose white and tall
In the valley below it, and thrilled to hear
The voice of the great town roaring near.

When the mountain stream from its idle play
Was caught by the mill-wheel and borne away
And trained to labour, the gray rock mused,
'Tree and verdure and stream are used
By man the master, but I remain
Friend of the mountain and star and plain,
Unchanged forever by God's decree
While passing centuries bow to me.'

Then all unwarned, with a mighty shock
Out of the mountain was wrenched the rock;
Bruised and battered, and broken in heart
It was carried away to the common mart.
Wrenched, and ruined in peace and pride,
'Oh, God is cruel,' the granite cried,
'Comrade of mountain, of star the friend,
By all deserted - how sad my end.'

A dreaming sculptor in passing by
Gazed on the granite with thoughtful eye;
Then stirred with a purpose supremely grand
He bade his dream in the rock expand.
And lo! from the broken and shapeless mass
That grieved and doubted, it came to pass
That a glorious statue of priceless worth
And infinite beauty adorned the earth.

Behold the earth swung in among the stars
Fit home for gods if men were only kind -
Do thou thy part to shape it to those ends,
By shaping thine own life to perfectness.
Seek nothing for thyself or thine own kin
That robs another of one hope or joy,
Let no man toil in poverty and pain
To give thee unearned luxury and ease.
Feed not the hungry servitor with stones,
That idle guests may fatten on thy bread.
Look for the good in stranger and in foe,
Nor save thy praises for the cherished few;
And let the weakest sinner find in thee
An impetus to reach receding heights.
Behold the earth swung in among the stars -
Fit home for gods; wake thou the God within
And by the broad example of thy love
Communicate Omnipotence to men.
All men are unawakened gods: be thine
The voice to rouse them from unhappy sleep

Sad man, Sad man, tell me, pray,
What did you see to-day?

I saw the unloved and unhappy old, waiting for slow
delinquent death to come.
Pale little children toiling for the rich, in rooms where
sunlight is ashamed to go.
The awful alms-house, where the living dead rot slowly in
their hideous open graves.
And there were shameful things;
Soldiers and forts, and industries of death, and devil ships,
and loud-winged devil birds,
All bent on slaughter and destruction. These and yet more
shameful things mine eyes beheld.
Old men upon lascivious conquest bent, and young men
living with no thought of God;
And half clothed women puffing at a weed, aping the vices of
the underworld -
Engrossed in shallow pleasures and intent on being barren
wives.
These things I saw.
(How God must loathe His earth.)

Glad man, Glad man, tell me, pray,
What did you see to-day?

I saw an aged couple, in whose eyes
Shone that deep light of mingled love and faith
Which makes the earth one room of Paradise,
And leaves no sting in death.

I saw fair regiments of children pour,
Rank after rank, out of the schoolroom door
By Progress mobilised. They seemed to say
'Let ignorance make way;
We are the heralds of a better day.'

I saw the college and the church that stood
For all things sane and good.

I saw God's helpers in the shop and slum
Blazing a path for health and hope to come;
And men and women of large soul and mind
Absorbed in toil for bettering their kind.

Then, too, I saw life's sweetest sight and best -
Pure mothers with dear babies at the breast,
These things I saw.
(How God must love His earth.)

Well, you are free;
The longed for, lied for, waited for decree
Is yours to-day.
I made no protest; and you had your say,
And left me with no vestige of repute.
Neglect, abuse, and cruelty you charge
With broken marriage vows. The list is large
But not to be denied. So I was mute.

Now you shall listen to a few plain facts
Before you go out wholly from my life
As some man's wife.
Read carefully this statement of your acts
Which changed the lustre of my honeymoon
To sombre gloom,
And wrenched the cover from Pandora's box.

In those first talks
'Twixt bride and groom I showed you my whole heart,
Showed you how deep my love was and how true;
With all a strong man's feeling I loved YOU:
(God, how I loved you, my one chosen mate.)
But I learned this
(So poorly did you play your little part):
You married marriage, to avoid the fate
Of having 'Miss'
Carved on your tombstone. Love you did not know,
But you were greedy for the showy things
That money brings.
Such weak affection as you could bestow
Was given the provider, not the lover.

The knowledge hurt. Keen pain like that is dumb;
And masks itself in smiles, lest men discover.
But I was lonely; and the feeling grew
The more I studied you.

Into your shallow heart love could not come,
But yet you loved my love; because it gave
The prowess of a mistress o'er a slave.
You showed your power
In petty tyranny hour after hour,
Day after day, year after lengthening years.
My tasks, my pleasures, my pursuits were not
Held near or dear,
Or made to seem important in your thought.
My friends were not your friends; you goaded me
By foolish and ignoble jealousy,
Till, through suggestion's laws
I gave you cause.
The beauteous ideal Love had hung
In my soul's shrine,
And worshipped as a something all divine,
With wanton hand you flung
Into the dust. And then you wondered why
My love should die.
My sins and derelictions cry aloud
To all the world: my head is bowed
Under its merited reproaches. Yours
Is lifted to receive
The sympathy the court's decree insures.
The world loves to believe
In man's depravity and woman's worth;
But I am one of many men on earth
Whose loud resounding fall
Is like the crashing of some well-built wall
Which those who seek can trace
To the slow work of insects at its base.
. . . .
Be not afraid.
The alimony will be promptly paid

For works with similar titles, see Dialogue.   HE

Let us be friends. My life is sad and lonely,
While yours with love is beautiful and bright.
Be kind to me: I ask your friendship only.
No Star is robbed by lending darkness light.

SHE

I give you friendship as I understand it,
A sentiment I feel for all mankind.

HE

Oh, give me more; may not one friend command it?

SHE

Look in the skies, 'tis there the star you'll find;
It casts its beams on all with equal favour.

HE

I would have more than what all men may claim.

SHE

Then your ideas of friendship strongly savour
Of sentiments which wear another name.

HE

May not one friend receive more than another?

SHE

Not man from woman and still remain a friend.
Life holds but three for her, a father, brother,
Lover - against the rest she must contend.

HE

Against the universe I would protect you,
With my life even, nor hold the price too dear.

SHE

But not against yourself, should fate select you
As Lancelot for foolish Guinevere.

HE

You would not tempt me?

SHE

That is undisputed.
We put the question back upon the shelf.
My point remains unanswered, unrefuted
No man protects a woman from himself.

HE

I am immune: for once I loved with passion,
And all the fires within me burned to dust.
I think of woman but in friendly fashion:
In me she finds a comrade safe to trust.

SHE

So said Mount Peelée to the listening ocean:
Behold what followed! Let the good be wise.

Though human hearts proclaim extinct emotion,
Beware how high the tides of friendship rise.

For works with similar titles, see A Wish.   Great dignity ever
attends great grief,
  And silently walks beside it;
  And I always know when I see such woe
  That Invisible Helpers guide it.
  And I know deep sorrow is like a tide,
  It cannot ever be flowing;
  The high-water mark in the night and the dark -
  Then dawn, and the outward going.

But the people who pull at my heart-strings hard
Are the ones whom destiny hurries
Through commonplace ways to the end of their days,
And pesters with paltry worries.
The peddlers who trudge with a budget of wares
To the door that is slammed unkindly;
The vendor who stands with his shop in his hands
Where the hastening hosts pass blindly;

The woman who holds in her poor flat purse
The price of her rent-room only,
While her starved eye feeds on the comfort she needs
To brighten the lot that is lonely;
The man in the desert of endless work,
Unsoftened by islands of leisure;
And the children who toil in the dust and the soil,
While their little hearts cry for pleasure;

The people who labour, and scrimp, and save,
At the call of some thankless duty,
And carefully hide, with a mien of pride,
Their ravening hunger for beauty;
These ask no pity, and seek no aid,
But the thought of them somehow is haunting;
And I wish I might fling at their feet everything
That I know in their hearts they are wanting.

For works with similar titles, see Justice.   However inexplicable may seem
 Event and circumstance upon the earth,
 Though favours fall on those who none esteem,
 And insult and indifference greet worth,
 Though poverty repays a life of toil,
 And riches spring where idle feet have trod,
 And storms lay waste the patiently tilled soil -
 Yet Justice sways the universe of God.

 As undisturbed the stately stars remain
 Beyond the glare of day's obscuring light,
 So Justice dwells, though mortal eyes in vain
 Seek it persistently by reason's sight.
 But, when once freed, the illumined soul looks out -
 Its cry will be, 'O God, how could I doubt?'

For works with similar titles, see An Old Song.   Two roadways
lead from this land to That, and one is the road of Prayer;
  And one is the road of Old-time Songs, and every note is a
stair.

A shabby old man with a music machine on the sordid city
street;
  But suddenly earth seemed Arcady, and life grew young and
sweet.
  For the city street fled, and the world was green, and a little
house stood by the sea;
  And she came singing a martial air (she who was peace itself);
She brought back with her the old, strange charm, of mingled
pathos and glee -

With her eyes of a child in a woman's face, and her soul of a
saint in an elf.
  She had been gone for many a year. They tell us it is not far -
  That silent place where the dear ones go, but it might as well
be a star.
  Yes, it might as well be a distant star as a beautiful Near-by
Land,
  If we hear no voice, and see no face, and feel no touch of a
hand.

But now she had come, for I saw her there, and she looked so
blithe and young;
  (Not white and still, as I saw her last) and the rose that she
wore was red;
  And her voice soared up in a bird-like trill, at the end of the
song she sung,
  And she mimicked a soldier's warlike stride, and tossed back
her dear little head.

She had gone for many a year, and never came back before;
  But I think she dwells in a Near-by Land, since song jarred

open the door;
 Yes, I think it is surely a Near-by Land, that place where our loved ones are,
 For the song would never have reached her ear had she been on a distant star.

 Two roadways lead from this land to That, and one is the road of Prayer,
 And one is the road of Old-time Songs, and every note is a stair.

Lord of all the Universe, when I think of YOU,
Flinging stars out into space, moving suns and tides;
Then this little mortal mind gets the larger view,
And the carping self of me runs away and hides.

Then I see all shadowed paths leading out to Light;
See the false things fade away, leaving but the True;
See the wrong things slay themselves, leaving only Right;
When this little mortal mind gets the larger view.

Cavillings at this and that, censure, doubt and fear,
Fly, as fly before the dawn, insects of the night;
Life and Death are understood; everything seems clear,
All the wrong things slay themselves, leaving only Right.

The World has walked with fever in its veins
For many and many a day. Oh, poor, sick world!
Not knowing all its dreams of greed and gain,
Of selfish conquest and possession, were
Disordered visions of a brain diseased.

Now the World's malady is at its height
And there is foul contagion in its breath.
It raves of death and slaughter; and the stars
Shake with reverberations of its cries,
And the sad seas are troubled and disturbed.
So must it rave - this sick and suffering world -
Until the old secretions in its blood
Are emptied out and purged away by war;
And the deep seated cankers of the mind
Begin the healing process. Then a calm
Shall come upon the earth; and that loved word
PEACE, shall be understood from shore to shore.

Shriek on, mad world. The great Physician sits
Serenely conscious of the coming change,

Nor seeks to check the fever; it must run
Until its course is finished. He can wait.

In his vast Solar Systems he has seen
So many other worlds as sick as this
He feels but pity for his ailing charge,
Not blame or anger. And he knows the hour
Will surely dawn when that sick child shall wake
Free from all frenzied fancies, and shall turn
Clear-seeing eyes upon the face of God.
Then shall begin the new millennium.

Lord of all the Universe, when I think of YOU,
Then this little mortal mind gets the larger view;
Then I see all shadowed paths leading into Light,
Where the wrong things slay themselves, leaving only Right.

Oh, poor, sick world!

Let us halt now for a space in our hurrying;
Let us take time to look up and look out;
Let us refuse for a spell to be worrying;
Let us decline to both question and doubt.
If one goes cavilling,
Hair splitting, flaw hunting - ready for strife -
All the best pleasure is missed in the travelling
Onward through life.

Just for to-day we will put away sorrowing -
Just for to-day not a tear shall be shed;
Nor will we fear anything, or go borrowing
Pain from the future by profitless dread.
Thought shall go frolicking,
Pleasuring, treasuring everything bright -
Tasting the joy that is found just in rollicking
On through the light.

Just for to-day all the ills that need bettering
We will omit from our notebook of mind;
All that is good we will mark by red-lettering; -
Those things alone we are seeking to find.
Things to be sad over,
Pine over, whine over - pass them, I say!
Nothing is noted save what we are glad over -
This is Praise Day.

The days grow shorter, the nights grow longer;
  The headstones thicken along the way,
And life grows sadder, but love grows stronger,
  For those who walk with us day by day.

The tear comes quicker, the laugh comes slower;
  The courage is lesser to do and dare;
And the tide of joy in the heart falls lower,
  And seldom covers the reefs of care.

But all true things in the world seem truer;
  And the better things of earth seem best,
And friends are dearer, as friends are fewer,
  And love is all as our sun dips west.

Then let us clasp hands as we walk together,
  And let us speak softly in love's sweet tone;
For no man knows on the morrow whether
  We two pass on - or but one alone.

Oh! that is a beautiful land I wis,
The land of the Gone-Away Souls.
Yes, a lovelier region by far than this
(Though this is a world most fair),
The goodliest goal of all good goals,
Else why do our friends stay there?
I walk in a world that is sweet with friends,
And earth I have ever held dear;
Yes, love with duty and beauty blends,
To render the earth plane bright.
But faster and faster, year on year
My comrades hurry from sight.

They hurry away to the Over-There,
And few of them say Farewell.
Yes, they go away with a secret air
As if on a secret quest.
And they come not back to the earth to tell
Why that land seems the best.

Messages come from the mystic sphere,
But few know the code of that land;
Yes, many the message, but few who hear
In the din of the world below,
Or hearing the message, can understand
Those truths which we long to know.

But it must be the goal of all good goals,
And I think of it more and more,
Yes I think of that land of the Gone-Away-Souls
And its growing host of friends
Who will hail my bark when it touches shore
Where the last brief journey ends.

All day, all day in a calm like death
The harp hung waiting the sea wind's breath.

When the western sky flushed red with shame
At the sun's bold kiss, the sea wind came.

Said the harp to the breeze, Oh, breathe as soft
As the ring-dove cooes from its nest aloft.

I am full of a song that mothers croon
When their wee ones tire of their play at noon.

Though a harp may feel 'tis a silent thing
Till the breeze arises and bids it sing.

Said the wind to the harp, Nay, sing for me
The wail of the dead that are lost at sea.

I caught their cry as I came along,
And I hurried to find you and teach you the song.

Oh, the heart is the harp, and love is the breeze,
And the song is ever what love may please.

For works with similar titles, see The Pendulum.   (In Edgar Allan Poe's story, 'The Pit and the Pendulum,' the victim is bound hand and foot, face upturned to a huge, knife-edged pendulum which swings back and forth across his body, the blade dropping closer to his heart at each swing.)

Bound hand and foot in the pit I lie,
And the wall about me is strong and high;
Stronger and higher it grows each day,
With maximum labour and minimum pay;
And there is no ladder whereon to climb
To a fairer world and a brighter time.
There is no ladder, there is no rope,
But the devil of greed has given a hope.
He swings before me the pendulum - Vice;
I know its purpose and know its price,
And the world's good people all know it, too,
And much they chatter and little they do.
I have sent up my cry to the hosts of men
Over and over and over again:
But should I cry once to the devil, ah, he
Would hurry to answer and set me free.
For Virtue to Virtue must ever call thrice,
But once brings an answer when Virtue calls Vice.

Bound hand and foot in the pit I lie
While the pendulum swings and the days go by.

For 'Mabel Brown' I never cared
  (My rightful name by birth),
But when the name of Smith I shared,
  I seemed to own the earth,
(I wrote it without 'y' or 'e' -
Plain 'Mrs. Jack Smith' suited me.)

My happiest hour, as I look back
  On times of great content,
Was when folks called me 'Mrs. Jack,'
  Though 'Mrs. Smith' was meant.
It was the pleasure of my life
To hear them say: 'That's Jack Smith's wife.'

One day I joined a club. They said
  That I must speak or write.
So I did both. I wrote and read
  A speech one fateful night.
It made a hit, but proved, alack,
A death blow to poor 'Mrs. Jack.'

As 'Mrs. Mabel Smith' I'm known
  Throughout my town and State;
My heart feels widowed and alone;
  The case is intricate.
Though darling Jack is mine, the same,
I am divorced somehow in name.

Just 'Mabel Smith' I can endure;
  It leaves the world in doubt;
But 'Mrs.' makes the marriage sure,
  Yet leaves the husband out.
It sounds like Reno, or the tomb,
And always fills me full of gloom.

They say the honours are all mine;

Well, I would trade the pack
For one sweet year in which to shine
    Again as 'Mrs. Jack.'
That gave to life a core, a pith,
Not found by 'Mrs. Mabel Smith.'

For one suggests the chosen mate,
    And all the joy love brings;
And one suggests a delegate
    To federated things.
I'm built upon the old-time plan -
I like to supplement a man.

If on each point of glory's star
    My name shone like a pearl,
I'd feel a pleasure greater far
    In being 'Jack Smith's girl.'
It is ridiculous, I know,
But then, you see, I'm fashioned so.

Amidst applauding cheers I won a prize.
A cynic watched me, with ironic eyes;
An open foe, in open hatred, sneered;
I cared for neither. Then my friend appeared.
Eager, I listened for his glad 'Well done.'
But sudden shadow seemed to shroud my sun.
He praised me: yet each slow, unwilling word
Forced from its sheath base Envy's hidden sword,
Two-edged, it wounded me; but, worst of all,
It thrust my friend down from his pedestal,
And showed him as he was - so small, so small.

SPRING

A sudden softness in the wind;
　A glint of song, a-wing;
A fragrant sound that trails behind,
　And joy in everything.

A sudden flush upon the cheek,
　The teardrop quick to start;
A hope too delicate to speak,
　And heaven within the heart.

SUMMER

A riotous dawn and the sea's great wonder;
　The red, red heart of a rose uncurled;
And beauty tearing her veil asunder,
　In sight of a swooning world.

A call of the soul, and the senses blended;
　The Springtime lost in the glow of the sun,
And two lives rushing, as God intended,
　To meet and mingle as one.

AUTUMN

The world is out in gala dress;
　And yet it is not gay.
Its splendour hides a loneliness
　For something gone away.

(Laughter and music on the air;
　A shower of rice and bloom.
Smiles for the fond departing pair -
　And then the empty room.)

WINTER

Two trees swayed in the winter wind; and dreamed
The snowflakes falling about them were bees
Singing among the leaves. And they were glad,
Knowing the dream would soon come true.

Beside the hearth an aged couple rocked,
And dozed; and dreamed the friends long passed from sight
Were with them once again. They woke and smiled,
Knowing the dream would soon come true.

There was once a little comet who lived near the Milky
Way!
She loved to wander out at night and jump about and play.
The mother of the comet was a very good old star -
She used to scold her reckless child for venturing out too far;
She told her of the ogre, Sun, who loved on stars to sup,
And who asked no better pastimes than gobbling comets up.

But instead of growing cautious and of showing proper fear,
The foolish little comet edged up near, and near, and near.
She switched her saucy tail along right where the Sun could
see,
And flirted with old Mars and was bold as bold could be.
She laughed to scorn the quiet stars, who never frisked about;
She said there was no fun in life unless you ventured out.

She liked to make the planets stare, and wished no better
mirth
Than just to see the telescopes aimed at her from the Earth.
She wondered how so many stars could mope through nights
and days,
And let the sickly faced old moon get all the love and praise.
And as she talked and tossed her head and switched her
shining trail,
The staid old mother star grew sad, her cheek grew wan and
pale.

For she had lived there in the skies a million years or more,
And she had heard gay comets talk in just this way before.
And by and by there came an end to this gay comet's fun -
She went a tiny bit too far - and vanished in the Sun!
No more she swings her shining trail before the whole
world's sight,
But quiet stars she laughed to scorn are twinkling every
night.

WHEN LOVE FOR HIS MAKER AWOKE IN MAN, THE DANCE BEGAN

The wave of the ocean, the leaf of the wood,
In the rhythm of motion proclaim life is good.
The stars are all swinging to metres and rhyme,
The planets are singing while suns mark the time.
The moonbeams and rivers float off in a trance,
The Universe quivers - on, on with the dance!

Our partners we pick from the best of the throng
In the ballroom of Life and go lilting along;
We follow our fancy, and choose as we will,
For waltz or for tango or merry quadrille;
But ever one partner is waiting us all
At the end of the programme, to finish the ball.

Unasked, and unwelcome, he comes without leave
And calls when he chooses, 'My dance, I believe?'
And none may refuse him, and none may say no;
When he beckons the dancer, the dancer must go.
You may hate him, and shun him; and yet in life's ball
For the one who lives well 'tis the best dance of all.

Since early this morning the world has seemed surging
   With unworded rhythm, and rhyme without thought.
It may be the Muses take this way of urging
   The patience and pains by which poems are wrought.
It may be some singer who passed into glory,
   With songs all unfinished, is lingering near
And trying to tell me the rest of the story,
   Which I am too dull of perception to hear.

I hear not, I see not; but feel the sweet swinging
   And swaying of metre, in sunlight and shade,
The still arch of Space with such music is ringing
   As never an audible orchestra made.
The moments glide by me, and each one is dancing;
   Aquiver with life is each leaf on the tree,
And out on the ocean is movement entrancing,
   As billow with billow goes racing with glee.

With never a thought that is worthy the saying,
   And never a theme to be put into song,
Since early this morning my mind has been straying,
   A vagabond thing, with a vagabond throng,
With gay, idle moments, and waves of the ocean,
   With winds and with sunbeams, and tree-tops and birds,
It has lilted along in the joy of mere motion,
   To songs without music and verse without words.

My Flower Room is such a little place,
Scarce twenty feet by nine; yet in that space
I have met God; yea, many a radiant hour
Have talked with Him, the All-Embracing-Cause,
About His laws.
And He has shown me, in each vine and flower
Such miracles of power
That day by day this Flower Room of mine
Has come to be a shrine.

Fed by the self-same soil and atmosphere
Pale, tender shoots appear
Rising to greet the light in that sweet room.
One speeds to crimson bloom;
One slowly creeps to unassuming grace;
One climbs, one trails;
One drinks the light and moisture;
One exhales.

Up through the earth together, stem by stem
Two plants push swiftly in a floral race;
Till one sends forth a blossom like a gem;
And one gives only fragrance
In a seed
So small it scarce is felt within the hand.
Lie hidden such delights
Of scents and sights,
When by the elements of Nature freed,
As Paradise must have at its command.

From shapeless roots and ugly bulbous things
What gorgeous beauty springs!
Such infinite variety appears
A hundred artists in a hundred years
Could never copy from the floral world
The marvels that in leaf and bud lie curled.

Nor could the most colossal mind of man
Create one little seed of plant or vine
Without assistance from the First Great Plan;
Without the aid divine.

Who but a God
Could draw from light and moisture, heat and cold,
And fashion in earth's mould,
A multitude of blooms to deck one sod?
Who but a God!
Not one man knows
Just why the bloom and fragrance of the rose
Or how its tints were blent;
Or why the white Camelia without scent
Up through the same soil grows;
Or how the daisy and the violet
And blades of grass first on wild meadows met.
Not one, not one man knows;
The wisest but SUPPOSE.

This Flower Room of mine
Has come to be a shrine;
And I go hence
Each day with larger faith and reverence.

My faith is rooted in no written creed;
And there are those who call me heretic;
Yet year on year, though I be well or sick
Or opulent, or in the slough of need,
If, light of foot, fair Life trips by me pleasuring,
Or, by the rule of pain, old Time stands measuring
The dull, drab moments - still ascends my cry:
'God reigns on high!
He doeth all things well!'

Not much I prize, or one, or any brand
Of theologic lore; nor think too well
Of generally accepted heaven and hell.
But faith and knowledge build at Love's command
A beauteous heaven; a heaven of thought all clarified
Of hate and fear and doubt; a heaven of rarefied
And perfect trust; and from the heaven I cry:
'God reigns on high!
Whatever is, is best.'

My faith refuses to accept the 'fall'!
It sees man ever as a child of God,
Growing in wisdom as new realms are trod,
Until the Christ in him is One with All.
From this full consciousness my faith is borrowing
Light to illuminate Life's darkest sorrowing,
Whatever woes assail me still I cry:
'God reigns on high!
He doeth all things well.'

My faith finds prayer the language of the heart,
Which gives us converse with the host unseen;
And those who linger in the vales between
The Here and Yonder, in these prayers take part.
My dead come near, and say: 'Death means not perishing;
Cherish us in your thoughts, for by that cherishing

Shall severed links be welded by and by.'
'God reigns on high!
Whatever is, is best.'

It is easy to stand in the pulpit, or in the closet to kneel,
And say: 'God do this; God do that! -
Make the world better; relieve the sorrows of man; for the
sake of Thy Son,
Oh, forgive all sin!' Then, having planned out God's work, to
feel
Our duty is done.
It is easy to be religious this way -
Easy to pray.

It is harder to stand on the highway, or walk in the crowded
mart;
And say: 'I am He. I am He.
'Mine the world-burden; mine the sorrows of men; mine the
Christ-work
'To forgive my brother's sin,' and then to live the Christ-part
and never to shirk.
It is hard for you and me
To be religious this way,
Day after day.

But God is no longer in heaven; we drove Him out with our
prayers,
Drove Him out with our sermons and creeds, and our endless
plaints and despairs.
He came down over the borders, and Christ, too, came along;
They are looking the whole world over to see just what is
wrong.
God has grown weary of hearing His praises sung on earth;
And Jesus is weary of hearing the story about His birth;
And the way to win Their favour, that is surer than any other,
Is to join in a song of Brotherhood and praises of one another.

No; God is no longer in heaven; He has come down on earth
to see
That nothing is wrong with the world He made; the wrong is

in you and me.
 He meant the earth for a garden-spot, where mill and factory stand;
 Childhood, he meant for growing-time - but look at the toiling band!
 Woman was meant for mother and mate - now look at the slaves of lust.
 And the good folks shake their heads and say, 'We must pray to God and trust.'
 God has a billion books of our prayers unopened upon his shelves,
 For the things we are begging Him to do, He wants us to do ourselves.

Jehovah, Jesus, and each soul in space
   Are one and undividable. Until
We see God shining in each neighbour's face
And find Him in ourselves and hail Him there,
What use is prayer?
   Let us be still.
How can we love the whole and not each part?
How worship God, and harbour in the heart
Hate of God's members - for all men are that.
Too long our souls have sat,
Like poor blind beggars at the door of God.
   He never made a beggar - we are kings!

Let us rise up, for it is time we trod
   The mountain-tops; time that we did the things
We have so long asked God to do.
He waits for you
To look deep in your brother's eyes and see
   The God within;
To hear you say 'Lo, thou art He; Lo, thou art He.'
This is the only way to end all sin,
The difficult, one way.

A prayer without a deed is an arrow without a bow-string;
A deed without a prayer is a bow-string without an arrow.
The heart of a man should be like a quiver full of arrows,
And the hand of a man should be like a strong bow strung for action.
The heart of a man should keep his arrows ever ascending,
And the hand and the mind of a man should keep at a work
unending.

Now what were the words of Jesus,
And what would He pause and say,
If we were to meet in home or street
The Lord of the world to-day?
Oh, I think He would pause and say,
'Go on with your chosen labour;
Speak only good of your neighbour;
Widen your farms, and lay down your arms,
Or dig up the soil with each sabre.'

Now what were the answer of Jesus
If we should ask for a creed
To carry us straight through the wonderful gate
When soul from body is freed?
Oh, I think He would give us this creed:
'Praise God, whatever betide you;
Cast joy on the lives beside you;
Better the earth, by growing in worth,
With love as the law to guide you.'

Now what were the answer of Jesus
If we should ask Him to tell
Of the last great goal of the homing soul,
Where each of us hopes to dwell.
Oh, I think it is this He would tell:
'The soul is the builder - then wake it;
The mind is the kingdom - then take it;
And thought upon thought let Eden be wrought,
For heaven will be what you make it.'

For works with similar titles, see Faith. Let a valiant Faith
cross swords with Death,
  And Death is certain to fall;
For the dead arise with joy in their eyes -
  They were not dead at all.
If this were only a world of chance,
  Then faith, with its strong white spark
Could burn through the sod and fashion a God,
  And set Him to shine in the dark.

So in troublesome days, and in shadowy ways,
  In the dire and difficult time,
We must cling, we must cling to our Faith, and bring
  Our courage to heights sublime.
It is not a matter of hugging a creed
  That will lift us up to the light,
But in keeping our trust that Love is just,
  And that whatever is, is right.

When the hopes of this world into chaos are hurled,
  And the devil seems running the earth,
When the bad folks stay and the good pass away,
  And greed fares better than worth,
Oh, that is the hour to trust in the Power
  That will straighten the tangle out;
For death and sorrow are little things,
  But a terrible thing is doubt.

For he who climbs to say his prayer
Meets half way the descending Grace.

ELSA BARKER, in *British Review.*

This is the secret of all prayers
    That in God's sight have worth,
They must be uttered from the stairs
    That wind away from earth;
And he who mounts to speak the word,
He shall be heard. He shall be heard.

And he who will not leave himself,
    But stays down with his cares,
Or with his thoughts of pride and pelf,
    Though loud and long his prayers,
Beyond earth's dome of arching skies
They shall not rise. They shall not rise.

Oh, ye who seek for strength and power
    Seek first some quiet spot,
And fashion through a silent hour
    Your stairway, thought by thought;
Then climb, and pray to God on high:
He shall reply. He shall reply.

For works with similar titles, see Answer.

Up to the gates of gleaming Pearl,
There came the spirit of a girl,
And to the white-robed Guard she said:
'Dear Angel, am I truly dead?
Just yonder, lying on my bed,
I heard them say it; and they wept.
And after that, methinks I slept.
Then when I woke, I saw your face,
And suddenly was in this place.
It seems a pleasant place to be,
Yet earth was fair enough to me.
What is there here, to do, or see?
Will I see God, dear Angel, say?
And is He very far away?'

The Angel said, 'You are in truth
What men call dead. That word to youth
Is full of terror; but it means
Only a change of tasks, and scenes.
You have been brought to us because
Of certain ancient karmic laws
Set into motion æons gone.
By us you will be guided on
From plane to plane, and sphere to sphere,
Until your tasks are finished here.
Then back to earth, the home of man,
To work again another span.'

'But, Angel, when will I see God?'

'After the final path is trod;
After you no more long, or crave,
To see, or hear, or own, or have
Aught beside - HIM. Then shall His face
Reveal itself to you in space.
And you shall find yourself made one

With that Great Sun, behind the sun.
Child, go thy way inside the gate,
Where many eager loved ones wait.
Death is but larger life begun.'

For works with similar titles, see A Vision.
My soul beheld a vision of the Master:
 Methought He stood with grieved and questioning eyes,
Where Freedom drove its chariot to disaster
 And toilers heard, unheeding, toilers' cries.
Where man withheld God's bounties from his neighbour,
 And fertile fields were sterilised by greed;
Where Labour's hand was lifted against labour,
 And suffering serfs to despots turned when freed.

Majestic rose tall steeple after steeple;
 Imperious bells called worshippers to prayer;
But as they passed, the faces of the people
 Were marred by envy, anger and despair.
'Christ the Redeemer of the world has risen,
 Peace and good will,' so rang the major strain;
But forth from sweat-shops, tenement and prison
 Wailed minor protests, redolent with pain.

Methought about the Master, all unseeing,
 Fought desperate hosts of striking clan with clan,
Their primal purpose, meant for labour's freeing,
 Sunk in vindictive hate of man for man.
Pretentious Wealth, in unearned robes of beauty,
 Flung Want a pittance from her bulging purse,
While ill-paid Toil went on dull rounds of duty,
 Hell in her heart, and on her lips a curse.

Then spoke the Christ (so wondrous was my vision)
 (Deep, deep, His voice, with sorrow's cadence fraught):
'This world to-day would be a realm elysian
 Had my disciples lived the love I taught.
Un-Christlike is the Christian creed men fashion
 Who kneel to worship, and who rise to slay.
Profane pretenders of my holy Passion,
 Ye nail Me newly to the cross each day.'

For works with similar titles, see The Second Coming.

How will Christ come back again,
How will He be seen, and where,
  Where His chosen way?
Will He come in dead of night,
Shining in His robes of light,
  Or at dawn of day?

Will it be at Christmas time,
When the bells are all achime,
  That He is re-born?
Or will He return and bring
Wide and wondrous wakening
  On some Easter morn?

When will this sad world rejoice,
Listening to that golden voice
  Speaking unto men?
Lives there one who yet shall cry
Loud to startled passers-by -
  'Christ has come again?'

List the answer - Christ is here!
Seek and you shall find him near -
  Dwelling on the earth.
By the world's awakened thought,
This great miracle is wrought,
  This the second birth.

While you wonder where and now
Christ shall come - behold him now,
  Patient, loving, meek.
Looking from your neighbour's eyes,
Or in humble toiling guise -
  Lo! the Christ you seek.

Look for him in human hearts,

In the shops, and in the marts,
  And beside your hearth.
Search and speak the watchword Love,
And the Christ shall rise and prove
  He has come to earth.

Sorrowful ofttimes is He
That we have not eyes to see,
  Have not ears to hear,
As we call to Him afar,
Out beyond some distant star,
  While He stands so near.

Seek Him, seek Him, where He dwells,
Chime the voices of the bells
  On the Christmas air.
Christ has come to earth again,
He is in the hearts of men,
  Seek and find him there.

THE END

Made in the USA
Las Vegas, NV
14 February 2024

85664784R00059